The
MAGICAL
FLOWER

Adaptation from the animated series: Anne Paradis
Illustrations: Guru Animation Studio Ltd.

CRACKBOOM!

True and Bartleby are going to castle-sit for the Rainbow King while he is away at the Neverending Chit-Chat Council.

"Above all, I want you to take care of my precious magical flower, the *Flowerus Magnificus,* which is in the greenhouse. Admire its beauty, but best not to touch it," the Rainbow King warns.

"We'll be careful," True says. "See you later, Your Majesty."

Not long after, Grizelda arrives at the castle with her dog, Frookie.

"Hi, True! Princesses like me also have to go to the Neverending Chit-Chat, or whatchamacallit, too. Can I leave my Frookie-kins with you while I'm away?"

True is delighted, but Bartleby isn't.

Bartleby gets jealous when True plays ball with Frookie. When True goes to get some water for the dog, Bartleby tries to get rid of Frookie by throwing his ball as far away as possible.

When True comes back, she asks, "Where's Frookie?"

"I don't know," says Bartleby. They go to search for Frookie.

They spot Frookie in the greenhouse. He's heading straight for the magical flower. His ball is right on it.

"No, Frookie!" shouts True. But Frookie doesn't listen. He jumps on the flower, and it releases a cloud of pollen. Frookie sneezes and turns into two Frookies.

"Oh, no — double Frookie!" Bartleby exclaims.

Several sneezes later, five Frookies run out of the greenhouse and wreak havoc throughout the castle. "The Frookies are going to destroy everything in their path! I need help from the Wishes," True says.

While Bartleby tries to capture all of the Frookies, True calls Cumulo to take her to the Wishing Tree.

At the Wishing Tree, True explains the problem to Zee. "Let's sit and have a think about this."

True and Zee sit down on the mushrooms. They each take a deep breath.

"I need to round up all the Frookies and turn them back into one again," True says.

"The Wishing Tree has heard you, True," Zee says. "It's time to get your three Wishes."

WISHING TREE, WISHING TREE, PLEASE SHARE YOUR WONDERFUL WISHES WITH ME.

The Wishes wake up and spin around True.
Three Wishes stay with True, and the others return
to the Wishing Tree.

"Very interesting Wishes," Zee says.
"I can tell you more about their powers.
Let's check the Wishopedia."

SYZER
can make objects bigger or smaller.

JOINER
can make several objects into one.

FLOTO
makes very big bubbles that you can float around in.

Snap your fingers to get it to stop.

"Thank you, Zee. And thank you, Wishing Tree, for sharing your Wishes with me," True says, as she leaves with the Wishes in her pack.

In the meantime, Bartleby has cornered all the Frookies in the kitchen.
True comes back and lures the Frookies into a pot with some Fishy Poof Crackers.

True activates her first wish!

ZIP ZAP ZOO!

"I choose you. Wake up, Joiner! Wish Come True!" True says. "Let's join all the Frookies into one again!"

It works! Only one Frookie comes out of the pot.

Grizelda returns to the castle.
True hands Frookie back to her and says,
"He was such a good little doggy".

When Bartleby hears this, he gets jealous, and kicks a nearby
ball down the hall. Frookie jumps out of Grizelda's arms and
runs after it.

Frookie chases the ball back into the greenhouse only to bump into the magical flower. A petal falls on his head. Suddenly, Frookie grows huge! Oh, no! Giant Frookie starts to run around the castle. Bartleby locks the greenhouse door and tosses away the key.

"We've got to stop him!" says True.
She activates Syzer, but she doesn't stop it
in time. Frookie is tiny now.
Mini-Frookie bounces out of Grizelda's hands and
goes right through the greenhouse door's keyhole.

Oh, no! The door is locked! What can True do?

Luckily, Syzer is able to help! It shrinks True and Bartleby so they can pass through the keyhole, too. They quickly capture Frookie. But they have to figure how to return to their normal size.

"I have an idea," says True. "Floto can bring us close to the magical flower. Touching one of its petals should make us our normal size again."

ZIP ZAP ZOO!

"I choose you.
Wake up, Floto!
Wish Come True!"

From inside Floto's bubble, True, Bartleby, and Frookie reach out and touch one of the magical flower's petals. It works! They go back to their normal size.

"My Frookie-kins," says Grizelda, hugging him.
But Bartleby feels guilty. He knows he's responsible for Frookie's misadventures. True explains that he will always be her best friend, even if she sometimes plays with others.

"Paw promise?" Bartleby asks.
"Paw promise," True answers,
and hugs him tight.

When the Rainbow King returns to the castle, True tells him, "There was a little accident with your flower, Your Highness. It lost some petals."

The Rainbow King rushes to the greenhouse.

"But that's wonderful!" the Rainbow King says. "It means that she's going to bloom."

And right before their eyes, the flower majestically opens up. To celebrate, the King suggests that they all go sock sliding in the castle.

"Paw-some!" Bartleby purrs.
"The more the merrier."

CrackBoom! Books is an imprint of Chouette Publishing (1987) Inc.

Text: adaptation by Anne Paradis of the animated series TRUE AND THE RAINBOW KINGDOM™/MC, produced by Guru Studio.
All rights reserved.
Original script written by Doug Sinclair
Original episode #102: Frookie Sitting

Illustrations: © GURU STUDIO. All Rights Reserved.

Chouette Publishing would like to thank the Government of Canada and SODEC for their financial support.

Bibliothèque et Archives nationales du Québec and Library and Archives Canada cataloguing in publication

Paradis, Anne 1972-,

[Fleur magique. English]
The magical flower/adaptation, Anne Paradis; illustrations, Guru Animation Studio Ltd.

(True and the rainbow kingdom)
Translation of: La fleur magique.
Target audience: For children aged 3 and up.

ISBN 978-2-89802-034-6 (softcover)

I. Guru Animation Studio Ltd, illustrator. II. Title. III. Title: Fleur magique. English.

PS8631.A713F5413 2019   jC843'.6   C2018-942634-9
PS9631.A713F5413 2019

Legal deposit Bibliothèque et Archives nationales du Québec, 2019.
Legal deposit Library and Archives Canada, 2019.

Printed in Canada

10 9 8 7 6 5 4 3 CHO2067 APR2019